Musical Ekphrasis

Literary Vignettes
in response to
Contemporary Classical Music

ISBN: 9798451961384

Introduction

As a child, I began playing the violin at the age of five. I grew up in a world of classical music from playing in community orchestras to listening to my father blast Pavarotti's Greatest Hits in our home. It was a world of beauty through and through.

Later in life, I began studying the ancient Greek concept of ekphrasis – which in a nutshell is how art inspires literature and vice versa. I decided to apply the concept in a way that I haven't seen it applied before. Surely it has been done, as music has gone hand in hand with literature and art throughout our species residency on earth. Whether it has or has not, I cannot say for certain. Nevertheless, given my newfound curiosity about contemporary classical music in all of its cacophonical, arrhythmic weirdness - which practically all aside from snotty academics deem utterly unintelligible, I decided to dissect and illuminate its multifarious magic utilizing a literary tool born in the ancient world – ekphrasis.

I hope you will agree, it has been a fascinating journey. The range of possibilities seem as endless as one's imagination, well beyond the conventional boundaries of beauty. Listening to even a single piece a second time opens an entirely different narrative. An organic, raw, engaging, reflective, predictive, dire darkness and blinding illumination – all are potential crops of unclassified seeds sown in irregularly lined fields.

Contents

Okkyung Lee Bigly Fake Concert – Liquid Architecture

Steel carriages transporting souls leisurely glide past my window as oblivious to my presence as I to theirs. The exhaust from their movement a noxious perfume of smoke and gas. It is quite unlike the incense that follows their wake upon departure from their malleable carcasses whose inner scaffolding crumbles beneath the force of time.

Gazing dreamily into the skies above, I perceive an inversion of my own making as the great white whales gently glide over and under the planes penetrating their azure fields. Their forms contracting and bulging at sensuous intervals – only to dissipate into dew as the sun ushers in another opportunity for memory creation.

Thump! The three-hole punch pounds the remnants of once majestic pines bleached and whittled down to near transparency. A far cry from its days of racing alongside its kinsmen through an infinite sky, dwarfing its murderers below with their saws in tow.

Thump! The tire of a car descends into and out of a pothole on the street below. A momentary sense of dislocation for the driver, a tsunami for the microbes luxuriating in the asphalt oasis below.

Thump! I bang the desk before me, the chair behind me, the chair next to me and the lamp shade above me as a fly reminds me of my inadequacy to rise under my own volition above the ground upon which I stand. Thwarting the murderous intent of God's most menacing species, a sly breeze snuck beneath the barely ajar sill beside me and whisked my intended victim to safety – hissing a judgmental slight towards me as it passed by.

The curse bore fruit. As subsequent winds gently passed by in tandem with the traffic below, a bird here and there hitched a ride. One, slightly off balance apparently couldn't wait until landing and relieved themselves on the shoulder of a passerby below. An unamused urban warrior glared above when our eyes locked in an embrace familiar only to angels. Thump! The doors of my heart not only unlocked - they burst from their hinges, never to be shut again. Just as I rose to begin the ascent to collect my fate in my outstretched arms, a trolleybus kidnapped him. He hesitated, but his inclination to doubt overcame his passion to embrace and as soon as he had appeared, he vanished. The ensuing breeze carrying but a hint of the cologne which had instantly transformed from an intoxicant to a poison which would haunt me for the rest of my mortal days – or at least until I can unload it anonymously onto social media in the morning. Broken heart and crying emojis are a certainty – the modern balm for a ruptured soul (just as ineffective as prayer was in the days of yore).

The chaos swirling in tornadic spirals throughout my subconscious mirrored what was before me painting a scene of never-ending displacement. People sitting down, getting up, adjusting their chairs for a better view, sitting again. Opening windows, closing windows. Elevators rising and falling. Doors opening and closing. Birds landing, only to take off again. Clouds shifting from place to place as if even in Heaven one cannot find a comfortable seat in which to finally relax.

Just as the hours of day unwind, so does the time we have left to live. No matter how tightly we cling to our will to live, it unravels a little more every day. The shifting around us mirroring the deterioration within us. No matter how we brace ourselves with all our might against the wall of mortality, it will inevitably crumble into dust along with us. Our ability to sustain that melodious note whose pitch is ours and ours alone will linger in the memories of those who love us through the songs of the nightingale who will weave it into their compositions long after we have vanished into the night.

The passions of the day, like a flock of furies, hears the whisper of the horizon calling them back to port so as to rest prior to being unleashed at dawn upon another unsuspecting day. Out of our eyes, mouths, and ears they flit to and fro in linear chaos as a flame languishing towards its copulation with night who is beckoning them to follow her.

Our consciousness deteriorates in concert with the light of day. Our subconscious invites us to step into an elevator to ascend towards dreams or descend into nightmares from which we will be saved in the course of an earlier than normal, abrupt, morning resurrection. The buzzing of the boxes each transporting the unconscious sliding up and down the shafts of darkness create a sense of disorientation for both the observer and the observed alike. Just as a mother watches over her sleeping child, oblivious whether the child is at peace or experiencing subconscious terror, so too is the child unable to control whether the eight-hour respite from the responsibilities of life will yield hope or despair as one is forcibly led into the wilds of the subconscious.

The curtains are drawn, the doors open and we slip into an undefinable, yet oddly familiar bog. Slowly trudging through it as if driven to approach a scorching flame without a flight plan. An odd mix of fairies and imps tussle and bustle around my head, competing with one another to be the recipient of a slap. Nothing sticks to my legs as I traverse the bog like a transparent egg being slowly dipped in and out of a prismatic Easter like sludge by an unknown force. Only a trace of all befalling me will be left in my subconscious when the resurrection of dawn comes. A crumb with which to backtrack to yesterday's realm which will dissipate rapidly as the sands of a new day begin to spill.

Spectral rays emanating from without and within me stream across the eternal haze disorienting all inhabiting this world even further. The rays searching for one another in vain like trapeze artists rehearsing – one after another missing the mark, tumbling into the net below, only to be flung into the air to try again. At last they converge into a single coherent stream of non-linear images - humming like a beehive in synchronicity, thus depressing the cord to consciousness for at least the next several hours to come. Tonight's movie has begun.

Images flash by in a rhythm akin to my heartbeat. Seamless in form, but bereft of sense. Images shuffled like a deck of cards. Some fantastical, some nightmarish, others snippets of actual memories. All intermixed on an enormous palette of emotional hues - blended by invisible conjurers to either soothe, rivet, wrench or render your very soul. Respite coming only upon the opening of one's eyes, restoring breath to conscious reflection.

The pulsing begins to slow like a slot machine. The bog instantly evaporates as tunnels appear, each entreating the dreamer to venture in, like troubadours coaxing a drowsy damsel on the balcony. Into which will you plunge - obliviousness to the depth towards which you descend, let alone whether you will ever emerge. Breath held, chance taken, you plunge neither with or against your will, emerging amidst a new narrative as the portal from which you came closes behind you with the whoosh of receding waves. Silence. Worlds shift, bend and meld around the new fetus upon which it will feed until morning in symbiotic pleasure.

The rays of morning dart under your lids and begin the elevation, hardly a gentle endeavor. The ascension is laborious, as if a million fairies were tasked with rolling back the boulder before the dragon's lair. At the first hint of a crack, flies curiously buzz about the opening - seeking whatever treasure lay concealed from the carrion of night's evisceration of your most intimate subconscious sensations.

Still submerged, you begin hearing knocking. Not aggressive, but persistent. All of the elements of the newly arrived day have queued up before you demanding your attention. The more curious among them begins rubbing the crust from the rims of your lids - as if scrubbing a window in which one wants to see and be seen.

At last you are returned unto yourself and are fully alert. Thrusting open the curtains in defiance of death which has not managed to catch you through the course of evening's chase around the lands of imagination - you unwittingly, yet defiantly puff out your chest with a subconscious sense of triumph. The ethereal creatures of night dissipate into invisibility as the traffic of a new day ascends to greet you. Clouds of whales and carpools of aluminum fish glide and spit across land and sky as you get your bearings, having been horizontal for an extended period of lethargy. The light of day flittering between the venetian slats like pop rock candy exploding sweetly on your damp tongue.

A delicate chime pulsates in your mind as you envision the tasks for the day ahead. Allocating time for the necessary, anticipating the expected, and arming for the unexpected. In my parallel retro-active conscious she can see her grandmother winding the coarse sheep wool onto the spindle. The pulsating top beating in sync with a calm heartbeat, the volume expanding and expanding until the instigator is satisfied with its width. Then, bit by bit, hour by hour as the day unwinds, so will the spool as the coarse thread is delicately woven in pattern after pattern until the mosaic of a completed day of interwoven actions and inactions is complete.

A seemingly intrinsically meditative experience in the first moments upon waking - until one is jarred by something unexpected of course. The kettle boils and her heart quickens as it recalls the arrow wound it sustained but a day before. The memory rises to the surface as an all-encompassing, scorching ache that paralyzes one to all other sense of being. She takes a deep breath as she processes the image of the man occupying her most intimate space. Battling the paralysis which threatens to overcome her every sense of reason, she mentally wraps the image in a swaddling embrace which she tucks into a secret drawer of memories in her heart that no one but her and the captivating stranger have the key to.

With that she sweeps any cobwebs of distraction from her peripheral attention and confidently steps out into the world to greet all who are anticipating her arrival for participation in yet another day.

Galina Ustvolskaya Sonata No. 6

All night long we dug the tunnels deeper and deeper.
Loading pile after pile of dirt onto our backs as we
shimmied in rhythmic unison back up the hill to the
opening, only to be pelted by raindrop after raindrop as
we unloaded our burdens. A cathedral of engineering fit
for our queen.   As the night wears on, the maze slithers
side to side, deeper and deeper. The loads on our backs
heavier and heavier as we squeeze closer and closer
together as more and more workers join our ranks. The
queen herself is far from idle. Enlarging the colony over
and over again. An astute judge as to what is needed –
offspring generators, more workers, and from time to time
even a future replacement for herself.

Soon I will graduate to the rank of forager and defender,
my time in construction will be at an end. Boldly will I
guard our walls from all enemies who would destroy us,
repelling any who would smash our home. I will traverse
endless fields of grass, climbing over branches, avoiding
spiders and other towering monsters who destroy us
indiscriminately at any given moment - both with and
more often without intent. Harvesting the greenest of
leaves, heaving it onto my aching back I will make the
same long, perilous journey home.

My body is never at rest, but I have no complaints – one
cannot miss what one has never known or can remember.
I have heard that sometimes when someone is climbing
alone to dislodge food from its source, they have a
momentary sense of singularity which cracks open a door

to silence before they quickly rejoin the team headed back home.

We're heading to the opening, the alarm has been raised – a footprint from one of the towering monsters has been spotted near our position. We have only moments to spare, it has been raised and is incoming!

Outline for Violin Solo by Thorsten Encke

Nestled in the soft embrace of fresh spring grass surrounded by an undulating sea of colorful popcorn buds, seemingly strewn across the field by a rushing rainbow. I observe the frenzied shooting of palm sized balls of feather haphazardly into the foam filled sky. Bursting with youthful energy, they slice each other's flight paths forcing the others to pivot and dodge while letting forth a thrilling trill as they soar higher and higher as if reaching for the bell like the strongmen at the carnival.

The early morning rays unsheathed from the solar star mercilessly slash through the branches, both alive and dead, as they hunt for those attempting to avert their call to arms. My eyes closed tightly, I attempt to avert their sting, but to no avail. I am forced to face my last day. I can tarry no longer.

I feel a soft, tickling trickle down my cheek which seeps into my parched lips. So salty - how I hated salt as a child. Whenever they tried to sprinkle it on my food, I would shoo it away vigorously as if it were a flock of locusts.

I sense movement above me, behind me and within me. A tumultuous shifting and churning of bi-pedal animals all chewing on various concoctions of anxiety, regret, and indifference. All indigestible on varying levels - calm not being on the menu of the day.

All is halted as we assume our positions – the call has come, although none can claim with any certainty to have heard it. At the ready, the proverbial sense of tapping fingers on the table in nervous anticipation reverberates through my mind taking me back to the night I was waiting for a tram that would transport me to my beloved waiting at a café. It was running late as the ring in my pocket knocked my senses into a similar nervous frenzy.

Waves of sound reverberate up and down the line. Everyone always wants to have the last word – make their mark before departure. Ironic in that if none of us survive, there will be no one to recount the utterance for your posterity.

We clumsily mount the trench like toddlers straddling wooden horses. Clumsily lurching forward haphazardly towards a depression in the distance. Dying here or there makes no difference really. They'll all call us heroes back home provided we die facing forwards.

Our dodging sprint ends suddenly as a sulfuric cloud clasps us in a deadly embrace. All lie down as one. Silence slices through the dense cacophony of siege. Darkness reigns alongside a rising stench, reminding me of mother clearing away fireplace ashes in the morning.

An eternity later white figures appear slowly, hesitantly on the field. Methodically picking their way amongst the dead, discreetly chatting about this and that. Selection is key. Not all can be chosen. Soon, a new journey will begin for some of us.

Penderecki Capriccio for Violin and Orchestra

The Heavens opened and I was grabbed unceremoniously by my feet and ripped from my soft-shelled abode. Squirming about, shrieking in glossolalia, the conveyer upon which I had been placed began to move. The stimuli all around me sparkled and popped, caressed, pinched and slapped as if I were a shiny new Cadillac being prodded through its first car wash. If only I could stand firmly, under my own power, I could begin to sort all of these colors, smells and sounds enveloping me in a warm, snuggly, yet constricting blanket. One leg up, now the next. Like attempting to balance mushrooms on ping-pong balls. A momentary triumph, an inevitable collapse.

There is no point yelling anymore, time to contemplate one's next move. It seems I must face forward. It would seem impractical to face counter to the motion carrying me along. You'll never finish the race if you keep trying to go back to the start. If I calmly observe to my left then my right, I can compare the views and discard the inadequate from contemplation. Ah, looking above I see familiar eyes wet with happy tears. We've had a long correspondence these last several months. Lots of happy anticipation, some anxiety and a little fear of this our first face to face meeting.

Time seemed sweet, slow and satisfyingly digestible back then. Now as I look from one side to another that very same time is racing. It seems there isn't a second to digest even so much as a color before another dozen are jammed into my senses. The future handcuffs me to it as it pulls me forward – indifferent to whether its prey is shadowing its every step or being horizontally dragged against its will through the furrows of presence. No amount of protestation – whether lyrical or looney will persuade it to look back.

Like when one gets into a car and rides around unfamiliar surroundings, you become dizzy from constant stimuli piercing your conscious through every conceivable pore. A tedious calm prevails as the wounds sustained clot from the kisses as time heals all. Soon, the scenery all starts looking the same. Cities are cities. They all bear the human stamp. The only thing differentiating them are the experiences generated by the amount of quality and input you invest in unlocking their secret cellars. The first few attempts to break the seals are in vain. Only when subject and object are totally unblemished by sense of self can they be mutually open to a shared experience worthy of being deposited into memory. Like a pearl emerging from a cracked shell equating itself to the diameter of the pupil sizing it up.

Fate and will are bad dance partners forever stepping on one another's toes. No sooner have I drilled down on a singular compelling element of being then I am whisked away as the conveyor forever propels me forward towards the vanishing point whose distance away only it knows. As time and place shift shape and color like a kaleidoscope, do I too become upright, thoughtful and talkative. In infancy it seems as if a bag of precious jewels are dumped out on the floor to be sorted and sifted through as fate bejewels the staff upon which you will lean throughout your life – your character. Some sparkling, others rougher cut, some misshapen but captivating – no two staffs are identical. The spectrum of life's potentials all harnessed into a singular frame not dissimilar to the height of your own shadow.

After so much external stimuli one's ability to process and reflect on immediate surroundings is honed to maturity to the point it recedes to being a largely subconscious process. Alongside one's intellectual development, so too do your height and physical features peak as bells clang in applause of your successful summit. The cross section of your unique presence on this world in your given time is a combination of the conveyor gently easing you forward – like pushing a child on a tricycle for the very first time alongside the wisp of vapor gently rising towards infinity as you expel the contents of your soul for all the world to witness. Provided of course, they look up from their own concerns for at least a second.

A period of calm ensues throughout middle age. Domestic bliss, steadying careers, the typical ingredients of typical lives. All but the extraordinary few languish about in these tepid, still waters with little care that their timeline does not slow its pace to match them. For the extraordinary few, breezeless waters are akin to an adventurer's sense of impending doom as they see land in the distance but lack fateful winds that can fulfill their inspirations to reach it.

As you round the curvaceous bend of middle age, you begin to detect a choppier current beneath you. You can't see the drop off in the distance, but you begin to feel it in every fiber of your being as you begin to lose your grip on the oars. Thoughts melt before processing, words drip out of your mouth like baby slobber – without warning and impossible to detract once unleased to roam the alleys of nearby cochlear passages. Then it hits you – there is more glass than sand remaining in the northern hemisphere of the time capsule. While you were asleep on the job, the conveyor belt continued its procession. The scramble is on to tear apart your memories in search of lost puzzles whose pieces you had put aside in favor of languor. Like shards of lost time, you frantically struggle to assemble them into a jewel by which you can extend your morality beyond your death.

Looking backwards ever more often, I lunge for the past digging my nails into dirt well- trodden by my very steps - swiping their indentations as a rapier seeks to erase all trace of an enemy. Yet the trumpets of destiny call, and against my will, I am forever pulled forward no matter my desire to halt - or at least dampen its pace.

Acknowledging the inevitability of my name appearing on a departure manifest someday, I frantically realize I must hurry to put my affairs in order. After all, one never knows which breathe will be the short stick pulled that gets you a seat on the plane to oblivion. Sell this, trash that, put a sticker on this as to who gets it, throw that in the will to bequeath it. Next comes excited knocking on the doors of those you love, religiously avoiding any potential topics that might poke a hole in a hornet's nest. Non-stop chatter as memories pour from all pores it seems. A "good visit", even if it is a bore, is key. You hope their last memory of you is among the best. The number of visits you need to make lets you know whether you ticked all the boxes when it came to graduating summa cum laude in your efforts to court social acceptance.

Items sorted, loved ones kissed, it seems I'm packed and ready. At least I had hoped it would be so orderly. Such is "typical life" that the final drum roll sounds beneath your consciousness when you are preoccupied fortifying your legacy. Rarely is everything completed.

They will squabble after your departure, no matter how tight you pull the strings of the will. There will be those who will never forgive you, despite all your protestations. Others who you hoped would keep your memory alive, if not in their thoughts and words, then at least in their hearts, will more often than not forget where they put the matches for the candles. And worse yet, never feel a pang of guilt about it.

The conveyor stops. In those last micro seconds I fill my lungs with the deepest breath I can take. Fuel for the road as I dissipate quietly into the great unknown.

Faltung By Christopher Herndler

The calm after the storm. The wooden husk brimming with tightly packed seeds lists back and forth, undulating with each passing wave lapping up its tasty cedar belly. The damp, dark hull is fermenting with fear as pungent as the putrid expulsions we are squeamishly mired in. Desperate to slam the door on consciousness of our collective horror, we shut our eyes, try not to breathe through our nostrils, immerse ourselves in dreams in the hopes of deafening ourselves to the sonics of enslavement swaddling us in chains.

I dream of a morning just days ago, laying on my bed, marveling at a singular, thin ray of dawn peeking through the roof, winding its way towards me like a spider expelling its web. It strikes my outer lid and dissipates into infinity, never to be beheld again, slashed by the heavy steps of fate dragging backwards and forwards along the planks above me.

It wasn't but a few days ago – my brothers and I were gathered in a circle tucked in the womb of warm savannah grasslands. We had a small chunk of honeycomb we were passing amongst one another. The golden, sticky nectar coating our hands in sweet delight as we savored each drop. The light trickle tickled our parched throats with a delight beyond description. Foreign hides cloaked the footsteps of our enemy as they cunningly snaked their way through the tall grass in order to rip us from the womb.

Beaten, stripped and chained, we awaited our deliverance into the wooden crypt that would take us into an afterlife of innocence full of flames. Our hopes and happiness rose like vapor from our souls along that shore, escaping to hide in the walls of our abandoned villages, in the depths of our wells and the memories of those we would never see again.

The boarding began as we sluggishly dragged our carcasses back and forth, against our will, at the behest of people we'd never known. Just before disappearing below the deck, I looked towards the blank sky for any sign of hope. A single bird fluttering nonchalantly, drifting amidst the currents, oblivious to the cries of our suffering below.

It has been days, maybe months now. Storms have blown us off course on several occasions. The lines of our palms erased by scars, fate itself resorts to flipping a coin representing our collective – back and forth, as the ship lists in limbo. Which face will be the last to reveal itself? Deliverance or demise?

String Quartet No. 4 with Tape by Sofia Gubaidulina

A sultry June evening - heavily pregnant skies impatiently anticipating release upon those gathered below. An errant drop here and there caresses the crowns of preoccupied maidens clustered about the shores of fate. For tonight the currents will gently receive their floral offerings, and in turn reveal their heart's destiny.

Cherub toes gently dip into the cool, murky soup, slowly placing their floral wreaths into the liquid folds as if placing the swaddled Messiah into his stable crib. A small candle tucked into the blossom's bosom to aid in lighting the path to everlasting love.

The currents of Rusalka's den are unpredictable to mere mortals. Once released from the embrace of the maidens, the wreaths are at the mercy of the elements. Here and there, a rogue slurps up a wreath to whom it was not entrusted, diverting the path upon which the maiden placed it. Flames quiver as balance waivers. Water nymphs mischievously grab the wreaths from beneath encouraging occasional collisions and momentary dips, much to the dismay of their anxious creators watching helpless from the shore.

Amidst distant reeds an even more ominous presence threatens to divert destiny – boys. Slopping through mud, playfully smacked and spanked by rag tag, ring-a-round the rosie mashups of tall grasses and chatty nymphs - most blindly bound one after another to snatch random wreaths from fate's menacing embrace. Most carelessly toss aside anything in their path - toppling candles, sinking wreaths, tearing petals, tossing all about. Only a few quietly slip between the shallows, stealthily targeting a specific wreath whose owner's heart they wish to steal.

Maidens young and old, seeing the chaos, cast off the shackles of caution and frantically wade into the abyss - desperate to alter the course of destiny in their favor. Some dive for sunken wreaths in hopes of resurrection. Others slap blind waves, demanding their futures be torn from the greedy clutches of a particular knave they deplore. Fate is foiled for some, and saved for others. The steady course of the surviving wreaths disappearing beyond the future horizon, well beyond the grasp of maiden and boy alike. The ink irreversibly dried in their books of life as the sun turns the page on another day.

Amidst the splashing, laughing and thrashing a miracle transpires. His eyes meet hers. Deaf to the cacophony encircling them and blind to all but one another, time stops in its tracks for them both. Slyly she nudges her wreath off course so it is within his reach. He lunges for it with the enthusiasm of a fledgling taking flight for the first time. Her blush ignites his soul, scorching all sense of reason forevermore. Plucking the candle from the wreath with one hand, he extends the other towards her, leading her gently towards an unfamiliar shore - confidently releasing the wreath to resume its journey towards a fiery horizon. Fireflies kiss their cheeks, leaves drop to soften their steps, and birds of all species raise their voices in unison - tucking the remnants of day beneath a cozy dark blanket woven from harmony.   Four footsteps merge into two and eventually disappear altogether as they calmly sail the heavens upon the tails of shooting stars.

Hauschka at NPR: Mt. Hood

As bloody as a babe at birth, again I am expelled onto familiar cobblestones. Just as wobbly as the first time, I take a few tentative steps. I consume the dusk air as a starving beggar who strains to prolong the moment of satiation. Squeezing my eyes shut so reality can't seep in, I replay a familiar movie on the inner screen of my consciousness. The cimbalom gently rumbling, whisking curls of smoke like a concoction of fairies - brewing mischief in the vagabond den. Bloodshot eyes slyly licking the pearls dripping from the mouth of the blind chanteuse ill-fittingly wrapped in worn paprika silks winding their way around her sizable frame like a python in love. Thread bearing and wine stained, it's skin resembling gauze discarded from her audience's many wounds. For in her prime, her arrows had been sharp and never missed their mark.

Outside the den, time soundlessly chimed in sync with the waves of new faces washing up on our streets. Normalcy was devoured as the thirst for power rose. Our glasses emptying in tandem with their magazines.

The wasps snuck in through the loose lips of traitors, spreading like gangrene through a thoroughly gutted crowd. Dull were our blades bulging from patch work pockets. Filled in were the holes drilled haphazardly through our decaying bodies from passions and crimes of youth unleashed. And yet, we were a threat - the wait time for oblivion's embrace rudely slashed.

I needn't open my eyes, I can smell the ashes. I turn away from the past and head to the park. Sitting alongside the statues, I feel the ashes of my torn soul drifting like a gentle snow drift building layer upon layer of sediment deep within me. Many hourglasses have been shattered. Mine lay on its side.

Volumnia for Organ by Gyorgy Ligeti

Slowly he caressed the piano, as a lover the breast of their beloved seeking the heart's gentle pulsations. Fingers spreading like a lace fan casting its net in hopes of catching a soul igniting flame. The sensation of sound flowing like lava through one's veins as if poured by Macbeth's weird sisters from their fateful cauldron. The scorch of the candle soon melds into a steady warmth through which one's thoughts begin to breast stroke. Eyes close, breath is held, and hearing bypassed as all sensations muster their forces towards their singular concentration – the fan.

Thoughts continue their journey utilizing fate's, passing alongside a warm ripple here, over a wavelet there. A spectral path emerges behind the mind's eyes as colors imprint on the imagination at a metronomic pace. Some so all-encompassing they seem pregnant with potential for bursting the sphere of manifestation. Others pass virtually as unnoticed as common breath. All eventually converge into the sought for moment - the kernel of inspiration surges into the womb of imagination from which a note emerges. Opening a single eye, so as to capture the essence before the perfume evaporates, he grabs the quill before him and blackens the staff with genius.

A pregnant pause to savor the moment. Greed pokes at placid bliss. Not satisfied with a singular golden moment, fingers fumble ferociously for more. Clumsily climbing up and down the keyboard at disparate intervals with the right hand as the left hastily reaches for the surface to catch the muse's gasp before dissipation, frustration summits.

Such elusiveness! One can sense the elixir slipping in and out of one's clutches like tussling with a giggling gaggle of fireflies flirting with sprites in a sizzling summer twilight.

Exhausted, head bowed in despair, hands dangling beneath the keyboard, he pauses until frustration's storm passes. Haphazardly, imperceptibly, miniscule raindrops gently begin to prick the parched field, as a spider fumbles for the thread dislodged by an impatient human hand.

His hands rise. Emboldened by desire, dislodging the nails of sacrifice to mortal disillusion, they seek the bounty of freshly nourished fields of creative possibility. The fan unfurls as the ivory is boldly stroked. Showers of golden sounds merge his hands into a single page splattered with frenzied scribblings of sublimity.

Memorialization of a moment still traversing the bounds of time, his mortality and mine as they are replicated again and again by young and old seeking temporary elevation to indescribable ecstasy.

Having never encountered a keyless cage, Dodger began shifting his tiny frame with the agility of an octopus. One surmises the lad could well slip through the eye of a needle should he set his sights upon the task. At last, free of the inky bog strewn for miles across the moon drenched desk. Dusting off his dapper jacket, he struts with supreme self-satisfaction amongst the Charles's chestnut curly waves laying dormant upon his napping head.

"What a mess, indeed!" Dodger cried. Heaps and heaps of this and that. Some blotted, some not, others dangling on umbilical cords as yet uncut. Well, the night is young and Charles is old. Plenty of time for making the rounds, meeting new friends, and sliding some golden opportunities into one's pocket as chance requires of the artful.

"Who have we here darting to and fro amongst the tombstones of characters who might have been? Pip, do be more mindful of bleak English evenings. Has Joe never told you that nothing good ever happens in a graveyard after sunset?"

With a tip of his hat, Dodger extends a hand to Pip, whisking him off the page before Abel takes another crack at his fellow convict.

Off to Ebenezer who lay as dormant as Charles - a hollow corpse buried beneath a colorless shroud of tightly woven Egyptian cotton. Tinkling bells of hell wound about his neck and body, Dodger observes Marley slyly slipping beneath the sheets, looking for an opening through which to inject himself into Scrooge's dreamscape. Lunging for his legs, Dodger is too late. Marley has evaded capture, Scrooge's journey has only just begun.

"Excuse me, pardon me, do be so kind" Dodger quips with a gentle tip of his hat as he hops and skips over ink puddles great and small in his quest for the next adventure. A thick swarm of spirits and sprites clog even pinholes for stars seeking to penetrate the dense blackness of night. All in a hurry with this mission and that. Toppling one another in the frantic race to establish presence in dreams throughout the universe, that if successful, will be recalled upon waking.

By and by Dodger comes upon a grand gray house lit ever so dimly by a thin wisp of light. A heart imprisoned by its owner, beseeching a forgetful world to pause and not simply continue by. A challenge for Dodger of the highest order indeed. No mountains are as treacherous as those forged in the ever-shifting ashes of scorched passion.

Dodger nonchalantly shimmies up the cold iron railings like a silk stocking, only to be thwarted by unanticipated thorns lancing him from all sides, forcing him to retreat again and again. Shaking his head, about to abort, opportunity, as always, taps him on the shoulder. Dodger, sucking in his breath, giving us a mischievous wink as he snuggly squeezes through a shallow burrow with the agility of a rabbit just beneath the gate.

Wary of traps, he tiptoes helter-skelter - squatting behind rocks and ducking branches until he comes upon a window whose grime he quickly cuts through with a determined application of elbow grease. Peering within, he spied the odd mouse scampering here and there followed in quick succession by a roach or spider - dependent entirely upon which way you happened to glance. Swirling up splintered legs, darting across dusty wastelands of rotting confectionary and upwards towards dark chandeliers sprouting showers of crystal tears, they weaved an aurora of despair beneath the vault of a starless, endless night.

An irritable tap, tap, tap echoed in the distance as the bride's broken fan scolded the bowed head of her ward. Making his way towards all the commotion, Dodger felt a slight unease as the deficiencies of men were ferociously unfurled. Shards of words in a torrent of hate flooding the very corridor through which he struggled to make his way.

Miss Havisham fell silent as the shadow of Dodger's top hat pierced the cell's gloom like a shiv of sunshine into the tornadic belly of vitriol. Deflated, it dissipated into a whisper rising towards the vaulted high ceiling as Miss Havisham slyly grinned.

"Come now Dodger, don't be shy. Back for another night of merry mischief I see. I suppose you'd like to do a pub crawl with Estella, or perhaps it's my company you seek?"

"Whatever you desire madam, Dodger is at your service."

"So they all say until the task at hand is inconvenient. Nevertheless, take Estella from here - you'll serve me well by proving in droves the argument I just put to her."

Dodger dashed off, Estella in tow, randomly slicing through cobwebs emerging from the labyrinth upon a rectangular white shore, all strings detached.

Charles is entering into the deepest of sleeps as all churn upside down in the recesses of his mind. Waves upon waves of tears listing a great wooden ship towards its doom. Dodger yells, "wait!" but it is too late. Ham is on his way to save who he can, as he is a most upstanding man. Steerforth awaits, justice is at hand.

Peggoty throws a jolly arm around little Dodger. All will be well soon enough. Of this she has great confidence - for never has there been a morning when opening curtains that light, no matter how thin, of a brand new day has failed to greet her.

Dodger catches a few weeks atop a passing glacier of fog headed home. It settles upon the Thames just as Hexam sets out. Swirling about the milky soup, his boat gently nudges Dodger's dangling foot jolting him upright.

"Beg your pardon Dodger, I thought you to be a proper catch."

"Not tonight my friend, Fagin picked me pockets clean before I set out for the night. Many golden bobbers tonight?"

"No luck as of yet, but the night is young. Glad to have plenty of fog about, it makes picking daisies a little easier to hide from the neighbors."

"Indeed."

Charles had stopped dreaming for the time being and was simply snoring in rhyme with time as oblivious to the real world as he was to the world of dreams. Dodger lay back upon the fog nonchalantly gliding along the shore like a snail hugging a limb.

All was calm, at least on the surface of things. David lay asleep in the crooks of his books - eerie visions of Uriah floating ominously in and out of rips in his conscience, caused by alarms of reason desperately clawing their way out of the bottomless cauldron of momentary intuitions.

Oliver lay luxuriating in the singular sound sleep of his barely begun life, nestled in the warm embrace of forgiveness despite his being the source of the draft now wafting in from a shattered window.

Joe's caloric visions are as succulent and satisfying in sleep as his indulgence of their actualized consumption while awake. Even Dodger smacks his lips like a love-sick voyeur as he invites the cakes, pies, puddings and the like to tickle his tummy.

Whereas Dorritt's momentary, unanticipated naps here and there in the most inopportune places and times are less a product of gluttony, than of a life plagued by a series of indigestible hardships.

The serene moment was soon roughly sliced in half as cries of mayhem burst from the seams of revolutionary Paris. Dodger sprang to his feet and rushed to the court. The crowd's eyes bulging from fires raging deep in their empty bellies suddenly combusted in a torrent of bloodthirsty cheers. Dr. Manette pleaded again and again for the sonin-law his youth had unknowingly condemned. Frail, frantic, he was diminished to a mumbling heap of mute protestations – for all within earshot were deaf to reason.

Shaking his head at the mayhem before him, Dodger, knowing none would hear him, fled the scene only to be confronted with turmoil after turmoil ahead. Smike was being struck by Squeers, who in turn was pummeled by Nicholas. Oliver was being thrashed by Mr. Bumble as Bill chased after Nancy, as usual, through the back alleys of London - cosh in tow. But the pinnacle of fury lay in the eruption of truth as Sophronia and Alfred learn that neither was the catch of the day as promised by mutual friends. Tepid are the torments of Hell in comparison with discovering a long sought Treasure chest empty upon opening.

Dodger ran so fast he lost a shoe. Luckily, he remembered just who to turn to. Dr. Manette was methodically trimming the sole of a shoe. "It's a bit small, but it will have to do" Dodger said as he snuggled beside him. The poor Doctor hadn't taken leave of his conscious to repair in sleep, but he was nonetheless in a very dark place. He squinted not from the faint candlelight, but from memories pinching his every last nerve. Children dying before his eyes - abused, neglected, and exploited by the very elites to whom he had given his only daughter in marriage. How could he have forgotten? Was Charles really different, despite being of the same crust? Trickles of confusion stewed with regret streamed in broken tributaries down the old man's neck.

A Raven curiously bobbed its head in and out of the window, summoning Dodger forthwith. Peering out the window, he sees the throngs amassed. Trite slogans being chortled, snorted, spewed and spat upon the condemned crammed into carts parting their path.

The bewildered captives were jammed together like gum drops. This late into the revolution, all the wicks of the truly wicked had already been extinguished. The thirst of the crowd unsatiated, all that remained to feed them were victims of petty gossip, romantic jealousies and jockeying bureaucratic entrapments. Most cried out for mercy, others stood stunned - all knew their final journey had begun. The Raven circled overhead, impervious to the chaos, as Dodger watched helplessly - Sydney Carton was making his way to a far better rest.

No sooner had the blade fallen, then Charles awoke! "Run!" cried Dodger as everyone scrambled to make haste. "What's this mess?!" Charles confusedly cried. Papers strewn all about, ink dripping and smudging well outside its words. "Dodger, I'll catch you yet!" Charles dashed to and fro grasping Dodger by the collar and Estella by her skirt. Dodger slipped his grasp and Oliver too. "Clever little lads!" he cried as they slid this way and that - only to be plucked from the shadows all wriggling and writhing. Uriah cunningly hid behind Miss Havisham's skirts, but also to no avail. Miss Havisham having none of it, grasped him by the neck and cast him aside – decrying the never- ending evil of the lesser sex, of which he was a part all the while.

Much to his chagrin, Uriah was now wedged between Charles' thumb and forefinger along with David, Miss Havisham having given him the slip. A newly awoken Ebenezer opened his arms offering Charles a hug. Indifferent to such pandering, Charles grabbed him too by his enormous smile and dropped of them one by one back where they belonged. There were so many, he had to stuff them tight in that small blackening jar. Arms and legs dangling here and there, faces pressed up against the glass gasping for air. So many thoughts racing through Charles head. Running across the desk, up the walls, across the ceiling, into the bottle, out of the bottle and back up his nose. How could one concentrate with such commotion?

The door creaks open, Mrs. Dickens stands before him, tea in hand. "Good morning dear Charles, awake at last?"

Apollo's horses harnessed, the sun obediently marches towards darker pastures. In its wake tides caress shores collecting the remnants of another day. Granules showcasing all shades of brown from beige to black – born of beads of sunlight warmed blood - are nudged from their surroundings by destiny as they glide hand in hand towards oblivion. Billions of colorful specks remain - a conglomerate of continuing life. The departed continuously erode day by day as the bell silently tolls for each, only to be replenished upon Apollo's return to the joyful exclamations of new mothers. Depletion never leading to complete deletion of the entire species as the bell eventually tolls for all congregating on the shores of life.

Despite the ever-increasing anticipation of an unplanned, but certain voyage with time - many expend enormous energy in attempting to conjure the moment and means by which their departure will take place. Empty tea cups gently swirled in wrinkled hands, eyes bending scrupulously around each bend. Cards nervously overturned one by one – a Fool, a Chariot, a Hanged man in hands young and old with indivisible, collective trepidation.

As one watches the washing of the tides, sometimes the loss of a familiar one is a burden too heavy to bear. Mediums are sought, ouija boards despairingly fondled in the hopes of a reversal of fate. Just as IV's are injected into the soon to be parting in the hopes of stalling the bell for just a few seconds longer.

All dream of paradise. Ironically, few want to actually go there when the bell finally tolls for them. Perhaps their subconscious in the last moments awakens their innate skepticism often silenced in their conscience thoughts that paradise isn't always as it appears in the brightly colored brochures.

Horatiu Radulescu - Subconscious Wave for Guitar and Digital Tape, op. 58

I've erected a sponge fence around my aural perception, thereby eradicating the noise pollution of constant jabbering encroaching upon my personal space to little more than the far more tolerable sensation of chirps. Behind me, erratic drops invading from tears in the ceiling pound the pots and pans laid out to scavenge them - leaving in its wake the resonance of a chime so faint none but a fairy could be imagined tinkling it. Before me, in concert with the rhythms behind me, cloud tears streak the grimy, mildew window.

I needn't turn to the interior of the room in which I am standing - I can hear the hunter sniffing. Left to right, right to left – nothing left to chance. Even the smallest crumb will be a feast in these lean times. I wonder though, he has scoured every corner of this room for three days straight with no success. Is hunger induced delirium drawing a curtain on his sensibilities as it has ours? For we too venture to the market week after week despite knowing full well the shelves will still be bare. Hope springs eternal for those attempting to walk in the footsteps of Oedipus.

Crack! Snap! Lock! The culprit is caught. They must have set it out this morning. Such a cruel fate – it wasn't even baited. His attraction to it propelled by desperation drilling into the depths of memory for sustenance - bypassing rational processing whose alarm bells he will not heed, pangs of hunger dispelling breath into the last vestige of hope swelling in his rib-exposed breast. His frail cries melting into the streaks distorting our view of what lay beyond.

The days are growing colder. It seems even the sun doesn't wish to slip off its clouds anymore. A spider crawling along the ledge extends its extremities into the minutest of openings in the hope of escape from our dank dwelling, having abandoned its web to ruin.

The family talks and talks out of boredom. Their subjects becoming ever more mundane to the point of flatlining into little more than an irritating hum of no consequence. You neither remember the Alpha, nor seek the Omega of it all, knowing perfectly well the pot at the end of the spectrum is full of bones licked clean antemortem – not gold.

Even the winds rubbing up against our frames move on rather than seek entry. Green leaves thrashing about whenever the slightest gust is sensed, waving all their arms and mustering a rustle louder than lion's roar – hoping to hitch a ride upon zephyrs as they flee.

Bricks gorge on their own mortar like lonely lobsters in confinement, all in the hopes of dislodgement before their time. My own sub-conscience cannibalizes what's left of my conscious in the hopes of numbing my senses to the point that I will become blind to brutality, mute to mortification, deaf to the defenseless and tearless to torment.

Fragments of still born thoughts rattle about the inner recesses of my echoing mind like knucklebones. Tossed, dropped, picked up, and scattered with drunken clarity as we stagger down uneven cobblestone alleys in the darkest of days.

Thin blades forged of solar unsheathed, battle to penetrate the viscous darkness enveloping us all in its cold stifling embrace. A barely perceptible ray breaks free from the struggle and scrambles for safety behind my eyes - hoping for solace in the warm spongy folds shielded by my cranium. Seeing the impenetrable film of despair sealing my gaze, it humbly beseeches entry with a few gentle knocks upon my pupils. Not receiving an answer it knocks harder. Startled at the intrusion, I blink. Offended by the obstinance it tugs at my lashes, pries at the corners, and stabs at the lid over and over again until remembrance of our former love for one another bursts the dam of my soul and a stream pours forth, forcing my lids ajar again. Our motivations unite. I grab a towel to wipe away the gloom - but as I reach towards the inner lens to let the light in, it vanishes as if it never came. In random succession over an unintelligible stretch of time in the distance there is

a shot or two,
  a forceful knock at the door,
   a car backfiring,
    an empty saucepan carelessly
knocked to the floor,
     an extinguished life crumbles
into an obtuse clump of organic decay on
      a cracked sidewalk.

All rendered as little more than as a collection of indistinguishable dull thuds. After all they are far enough away to remain unseen, frequent enough to be unsurprising and effecting strangers whose existence has neither enhanced nor hindered your well-being. All can be thoughtlessly tossed into a bin and expelled from conscious consideration.

I am reminded of ice skating on the local pond as a child. Gliding effortlessly through well-worn grooves alongside a plethora of familiarity. Pleasant chatter intermixed with flirty birds melding into a sparkling soundscape as pleasantly digestible as fizzy soda. Round and round the typical path. From youth to adulthood, career building and child rearing - to death by sleep when your branch upon the tree of humanity has extended so far beyond the roots that water can no longer replenish it.

These days the ice is growing ever thinner. The familiar grooves etched by others fading. The birds have fled - familiar voices growing ever fewer. Sticking to the shoreline, you no longer boldly venture into the center. Cracks appear unexpectedly. You begin anticipating them with trepidation at every turn. They pursue you well beyond the banks of the river. No matter how you far you run or how well you stop up your ears with cotton they seep into your subconscious, expanding their colonization of your sanity day and night. The pond has burst its banks and begun its final siege to avenge all of its kin who have been damned, raped by hooks, trodden upon with sharpened blades and genocidally herded into pipes to be consumed into non-existence. The abyss that lay beneath us will open wide at any moment for its last supper.

Devouring the last of the hominids. None will escape –
even those hiding in cellars deep within the land.

Foggy By Michiyo Yagi

Across the steppes we flew, a blur of courage striking forth - a path of breathlessness in our wake. An arrow unsheathed, stealthily hits its mark squarely during a suspended moment of flight - the length of a child's first breath. The commanding thunder of our steps striking fear and awe in those for whom our prowess was the fodder of myths as yet unwoven.

As far as one could see, waves and waves of warriors smother the sun with a blanket of hot dust churned with tornadic tenacity by our hooves. Desperate to stave off imminent annihilation, the choking sun gaspingly pleads for the moon to intervene. Throwing a black blanket over its quivering flickers, the moon shields its lover - forcing the tide to subside. The sun given a few hours to recover its senses before mustering enough strength to emerge from the blanket, bursting forth with a new day. We too pause for drink and rest – nestling our thoughts in the laps of night's invisible spirits before igniting our determination to thrust further into the steppe's belly upon waking.

As our years wear on, the dimensions of our lives exponentially expand beyond the confines of the wombs from which we emanate – some more than others. For upon our sturdy legs, legends are made and tragedies borne home alongside the friends and foes who will spin tales along the way ensuring their deeds – both famous and infamous - are whispered and sung of by all generations yet to come.

I have borne the weight of the warrior upon my back from thin to thick for so long, the imprint of his thighs upon my sides have become an extension of my own body.   Our rhythm across the steppe so intimate - even the best aimed arrow would fail to penetrate, let alone divide our determination to rule all roaming south of the horizon.

Now, as we ascend into our final journey your hot breath upon the back of my neck grows thinner, your weight shrivels to that of a feather and our eyes no longer target our enemies, but self-reflect upon a new journey within from which we will never emerge.

Guero – Helmut Lachermann

They still came at quarter past nine to savor a gentlemen's evening of wining, gaming and dining. Synchronicity permeating the staleness of unaired, smoke infused parlors –

hearts beating steadily in tandem with Rolexes,
well-wound foyer clocks,
balls skipping about roulettes and
the drone of pleasant (albeit recycled) conversing.

Roulette balls rested as champagne bubbles lazily glided towards mustachioed lips eager to burst their bubbles, greedily gulping in-between repasts.

Chips were plinked nonchalantly onto the worn green velvet. Threadbare upon those numbers for whom luck had smiled upon in victories small and large in games present and past. The roulette was wound again and again. Chips appearing, disappearing and reappearing again - swirling about in a whirlpool of wealth.

Long ago had those barely treading water or struggling to re-surface well and truly drowned. Those on the top deck were all that were left. The depths so beneath them, they doubted (if even considered) their very existence.

Sneakily shifting like a thief amongst shadows, droplets discreetly descended from cracks in the ceiling. Stealthily nestling themselves in toupees and upon the rims of champagne flutes soon to be ingested were the tears of the disaffected and outright oppressed – both living and long passed.

Long had they streaked the panes of curtained windows and locked doors. Only with time weighing heavily upon the roofs did the foundations within begin to soften as complacency set in - obscuring memories of those they had wronged to earn the seat upon which they were firmly planted. The droplets kept pace and went undetected, biding their time for circles to close. For night after night as the midnight chime tolled another would succumb to the silent knock of mortality until at last there would be no more.

Phyllis Chen - Double Helix for toy piano and bowls

The sun lay unconscious upon the mat of another well beaten day. A church bell clanged in acknowledgement of the temporary cessation of hostilities. Most exited the arena to refuel for tomorrow's continuing mortality match in which they would yet again battle for breath in an increasingly polluted world.

During intermission, a bold, bright moon burst upon the eviscerated palette to usher in a night of productivity. Beginning with Yutu the rabbit - who practically dwarfed the craters upon which he stood. Aggressively he began pounding away - concocting more immortality elixir for his mistress, Chang'E, who had nicked the formula from her husband Yi millennia ago. Despite being banished and rendered a toad, her prodigious immortality still inspired many below to rip a page from her book and stay up a little later to work on their own attempts to emulate her elusive elixir in the only way they knew how – proliferating progeny.

Alongside these urban dens, rabbits darted about dens of their own as excited little girls with noses pressed up against frosty windows tried pointing them out before they disappeared. Down a burrow here, up from one there, they frantically flew with the speed and dexterity of a spider busily constructing a mansion by which to ensnare dawn's breakfast.

All the while, the little girls began swapping their grandmother's tales like trading cards, as the moon suspiciously crept eavesdropping into their rooms. They imagined rabbits descending into the earth landing on mountaintops of fairy lands below - whereupon they delivered greetings from the non-spirit world from whence they came. Some of the girls proclaimed the soft haired couriers were their very own grannies sprung spry from their chairs alongside the rising moon - only to be repatriated from the land of spirits as the spider finished licking his jaws following a most satisfying breakfast. After all, hadn't one noticed their fur coats hanging surreptitiously behind the door even during the sweltering heat of summer?

Flutter by Alex Mincek

Precariously perched, squeegee in hand, the worker dips into a clarifying elixir before vigorously applying it to the translucent boundary between you. Your back is to him, despite being face to face. Gazing through him, your mind is clouded by superficial concerns. Mentally you check them off your list of activities for the day, one by one – unconsciously mirroring his dips into the bucket:

getting so and so to agree to the terms of a contract,
edging out the guy in the corner office solely because it is bigger,
picking up dry cleaning on the way home,
evaporating pent up rage on muscle altering machines at the gym,
funneling any leftover traces of emotional debris through the bottom of a shot glass away from prying
        eyes, before putting the dirty laundry in the bin to repeat it all again tomorrow.

Typical thoughts for a typical day.

One moves clockwise while the other anti. You trudge through blank pages, sloppily spilling unintelligible ink in your wake. He dips, bangs, drags, and wipes up your tracks, rendering your steps and missteps invisible. Your mark has yet to be made. He steadily keeps pace with ensuing time. Should your mark never come to fruition, you will simply close the blinds and slip through the cracks of human history. In either case, when either life or mark is left - he will motion above, the scaffolding will shift, and he will move on to the next window.

Meanwhile, you sit back down behind the desk - back to the world, blocking out the sunlight. You can't see the cobwebs encroaching from all corners, because you're stewing in the dark. Muddled in mediocrity, yet careful to brandish a cloak of mystery before all who dare peek through your keyhole – inspiring a heady mix of fear, fascination and caution in all would be conquerors both lovers and foes.

Cool as steel, hardly differentiable from your beams holding up your self-erected cell. "Career driven" say all those around you. It's been so mutually rewarding not knowing them all these years. The temperature of your countenance counters that within - where clogging desert sands keep time backwards, rising each day evermore. Sinking ever deeper, you have neither well nor map offering you respite. Your spirit rendered as little more than a stagnating Stag awaiting the spit of a Barbarian roast.

The fog horn in the bay cuts through the moment, jarring your senses from their conscious slumber. E-mails continue their migration from outbox to inbox as you reward them with a treat of a few words before sending them on their way. But something has shifted since the call of the sea. A brick has dislodged - a ray of imagination is piercing through your gray, tepid skies. You look towards the window and suddenly you see. He is cleansing the carcass of societies' elite, in hopes of letting a little light in.

Peering outwards to see within you notice blue skies swirling above like gossips hot on the heels of a well-kept secret. The distant fog horn bellows again, bestowing sight upon the blind. Bustling about on the streets below are waves of humanity ebbing and flowing - a discordant mass broken apart by the blare of a car horn.

You're skeptical, comfortable in your cocoon - despite its being ensconced in an arachnid's pantry. You resume tending to the pigeon flutter defecating your PC's view of its handler. Suddenly the sound of the elevator alarm makes your flatlined senses spike. They're stuck again. Third time this week. It takes hours to free them. There is no wi-fi in there. Better hope you're stuck with someone you like. Better yet, someone you'd like to love. You laugh. You remember. Several bricks calve, the thaw has begun, more light bursts through. The window washer's squeegee is silenced. Gently pressing his nose flush against the window, he is determining whether it is time for him to move on.

Boxes of memories come tumbling down as you hesitantly pry open an overstuffed closet. A few moths flutter here and there amidst dried roses, dancing shoes with well-worn heels, and of course that little black dress with the ripped zipper. Boxes upon boxes of good times and bad. Tear-stained, unopened letters jumbled together with your grandmother's treasured recipe for pierogis scratched out on a stained napkin. Photo albums full of relatives loved and forgotten entangled by those "python" jeans you swore you'd get past your hips during the last great diet. Digging here, unboxing there - tossing aside, clutching with pride. You bravely venture upstream against the mighty currents of memory in order to reach the greatest treasure of all – a box at the top lovingly wound with a red ribbon bow.

Having found your fountain of youth, you feel the drizzle of doubt chilling you to the bone with paralyzing trepidation. What if hope stumbles upon unfulfillable promise? A second exile is far more bitter than the first. Hesitation gnaws at anticipation. The alarms of the morning from fog to cars to elevators blare one after the other in a sustained battle cry, urging you to use all your strength to keep the door ajar. Meanwhile, lunging red serpents from all directions strike over and over again at your heart's core, puncturing your courage and injecting poisonous doubts within. All in the quest to thwart your attempts to transcend all – past and present - forces tirelessly monitoring and prolonging your mutually consensual incarceration.

Back and forth, back and forth you push and pull, pull and push against your subconscious's awakened, yet ever weakening will. Conscious and subconscious suddenly attract rather than repel in an embrace so tight not even your breath can penetrate it. The war has ended, peace between opposing wills breaking out like a morning blossom.

As smoke and haze dissipate into wells of forgetfulness, the red-ribboned box manifests itself as an attainable quest yet again. In childish excitement you leap in all directions, grabbing, slapping, and poking at anything in your path in order to gain a foothold to the summit. All is in vain as you collapse in a quiet heap of ineptitude - cowering from the scolds of destiny which has so patiently awaited your arrival. Solemn dignity must walk hand in hand with a heart brimming with selflessness when approaching the oath upon which only you are permitted to tread.

You shorten your steps, take gentle sips rather than gulps and steadily work your way up the winding staircase – the stairs appearing one after the other as you calmly await their readiness. The higher you ascend, the closer together the steps – the toil on your calves lightening as your sense of purpose is rising.

The box has been reached. Ribbons are unfurled with the delicateness of a conductor's baton weaving air to manifest carpets of intangible beauty. Gently, you turn each page in your book of life – reminiscing about long forgotten events with a grimace here, a smile there - a tear bridging melding their paths together. Each page traversed takes flight upon landing, filing the skies with a thousand doves as you come to peace with each memory in its turn.

At last you come to pages yet to be written. Your thoughts cleansed of the cobwebs in which they were formerly entangled, you are filled with new found vigor and clarity. Pen in hand, you are ready to begin the next chapter, as your spirit drifts ever further away from your former confinement. The man washing your window moves on.

Dringen by Maja Mijatović

The pulse of crumbling nations converge at long last along the precipice of the abyss - into which their inevitable descent is deemed essential by judgment of an unforgiving Universe weary of human nonsense. If future lifeforms ever bother to reflect upon homo sapiens prior to their implosion, it will inevitably be determined that all was set into motion upon expulsion of the written word from the womb of positive possibilities into the canon of indiscriminate destruction. Alternate species doing a thesis on the underbelly of human communicative thought in the Earthen era from the beginning of formal communicative efforts, will find that mankind strayed early on from evolutionary paths open to them to wander about ominous thickets teaming with thorns. Armed with everything from sharpened quills to pounding keyboard – the uninspired, unintelligent and downright malicious complicitly entered into conspiracies. Hands dripping with hate, mischief, arrogance and the like for centuries took up arms to take on enemies imagined and forged since time immemorial by

piercing purified parchments,
striking silent stones,
poisoning pigeon parcels,
providing transport for predatory propositions via bar napkins,
and demanding demeaning deference on "honey-do" post-its...

all the while fighting victoriously under flags of anonymity for the eradication of thoughtfulness. A global wave of victims - past and present, targeted and collateral, lay in the wake of poisonous words.

Our post-human researches are likely to inspect a petri dish of the most toxic words preserved in our hard drives and archives from inception to extinction. Under the microscope, they are likely to observe something akin to a phosphorescent microbe attempting to part a rabid pack of hate with reason. A gentle comment here, a nudge to conscious there. The pack defending its turf, congealing in an ever tighter embrace of vitriol until all in its path is rendered blind to escape, deaf to reason and mute to protest.

No matter the glut of hate, there will always be an element of light – no matter how faint – that will survive. Our researcher will struggle to define that singular element. After all, hate is simple. It's plentiful, shallow and utterly transparent. It lacks complexity and is therefore incapable of self-masking. Its boldness is its greatest weakness – it has no element of surprise or enough fuel for a perpetual life on the lamb, because it drains rather than invigorates. Its vehicle for transmission greedily drinks the poison which propels it, yet at the same time corrodes it from within.

In contrast, light is elusive - as fluidly form shifting as an octopus. It strives for ever higher altitudes, its light blinding to those seeking it with malevolent intent, liberating to those who are not. With unbounded courage, it seeks the unsought – the quagmires, corniches, and crevasses wrought through calving where the forgotten, the maligned, and the terrified flee when under siege. Those whom society has deemed unworthy of recycling - discarded to the appetites of an insatiable, congealed mass of anonymous indifference and random outbursts of targetless hate whose sole power to dominate lie in its capacity to generate continuous bursts of vapid interjections.

Having penetrated behind enemy lines rank with hate as far as the eye can see and as deep as one's eyebrows, light quickly rises apart and above from the rest - a major note hovering above the cacophony of a minor key. Its primary power is in robbing the robbers of their words – untying their tortuous knots as one solves a Rubik's Cube in order to reconstruct the deconstructed and to diffuse diluted discourses both public and private. Snipping fuses and slicing bombs to reveal their apple-like inner core – the original fruit of knowledge to be digested humbly, in reverence to the euphoric elucidation of knowledge imparted by its juices which enable the pure of heart to rival the cognitive capacity of an all-knowing God.

Despite being wildly outnumbered, light is doggedly persistent in breaking the will of the siege. Often steadfastly silent, its saber housed in a sheath of dignity. Maintaining its elevation above the crowd, however slight, its strength multiplies as slowly it rises, scooping up convert after convert until they collectively dissipate into oblivion leaving a single ray of hope in its wake.

Scaglie di mare for Harp by Ada Gentile

The tiny empress to be hobbled on unsteady feet towards a magical pond. Plopping down beside it, in a most unceremonious heap of endlessly jiggling, giggling, slobbering babyness, she stared in awe at what lay beneath. Smooth, shimmering sheaths of gold slicing through still, emerald waters - while a handmaid is smoothing down cascading silken robes slithering in the wake of her queen's measured steps. The empress sloppily slaps the water - startled that her hand slips through its surface and yet is still visible in the world beyond. The fish, jolted by the sudden clap of thunder emanating from its ruptured ceiling frantically darts about blindly in search of an undisturbed cove. Violently bumping its head at one juncture, its tail at another – the realization of its current vastly diminished proportions in contrast to the boundless springs of its inception becoming ever more apparent.

The empress, entranced by her newly discovered power dips a finger back in and swirls it about at a furious pace creating a glittering whirlpool – a swirling constellation of sparkling light reflections courtesy of a beaming midday sun. His head banging against the furthest corner of the enclosure in a vain pursuit of miraculous penetration, he confusedly spins around, gazing up at the dazzling tornadic storm headed his way. Instinctively diving to the very bottom and shimmying across its cool slimy surface like a combat soldier under fire, he manages to evade her best attempts to ruin his day. Not to be outdone, the empress grabs a small twig laying alongside her. Dipping it into random crevices here and there, attempting to turn her twig into a diving rod to pinpoint her treasure's lair.

From a window nearby, her mother coldly observing her progeny, loses sight of the servant who in turn slips away to brief the Emperor about her. Initially envious of her child's freedom to roam as she pleases, she soon snarls with delight when realizing the game with which her daughter is victoriously engaged is that of captor and prisoner. Tapping the porcelain cup imprisoned in her grasp, her fingernails beating in sync with plots cultivating in her ever-darkening mind - her confidence growing that her aspirations may be more readily realized in much smaller hands.

Plotting this scenario and that she begins mentally knotting snares, lighting matches and amid a grand concoction of devious traps. Thinking to herself, "the child is young, but moldable as clay. With carefully measured drops of poison slipped into her ear, she'll soon prove an invaluable weapon in overturning her father's opulent table and empowering her mother."

The little empress soon weary of exerting careless energy, lay down alongside the pond to indulge in a little sleepless dreaming. Sensing peace at last the fish cautiously emerged from hiding. The pure essence emanating from his golden soul hitched a ride on a sunbeam and rode into her heart by way of her eye. A fraternity sealed between them therein by her innocent smile, its ember now an eternal flame within her destined to withstand the endless torments from all sides to come.

Pression by Helmut Lachenmann

Surreptitiously it inched its way into the concrete carcasse's apex upon whose back the sludge of another day's workplace carnage noisily drains into yet another starless night. The bearing down of fossil fueled steel coffins, at first intermittent, increases in direct proportion to the annihilation of light – rendering the makeshift cradle beneath an insomniac's paradise.

Whether it was man or woman, adult or child, young or old was completely unintelligible - and to the world at large unworthy of note. A form rendered pliable, having weathered countless storms, it appeared boneless slipping beneath an eve mere inches in width before expanding to occupy the crawlspace within from corner to corner in a tortuously self-constrictive, suffocative positioning - reminiscent of a malformed babe in womb surreptitiously eluding society's abortive scalpel in constant quest of its erasure. The only sign of life - a faint pulse, unintelligible even to its owner, whose thready beats are in tandem to a digital neon clock flashing at the gas station entrance below. The sight of whose constant secondly progression being the only true indicator to all who noted its presence, that indeed time was still passing – thereby confirming their passive existence in it. Cognizance of said fact meant that one was still inside the blue egg and had yet to be well and truly expelled. Perhaps in a form beyond recognition from the person you might have been – whether travelling in the cars above or nestled in the overpasses below - but a living being nonetheless. And where there is breath, there is hope that life will one day be emulative of the paradisiacal myths created by those who endure it for the express purpose of fashioning a mattress upon which to fall when inevitable blows strike them.

The night is suffocatingly balmy. A ceaseless, putrid trickle drips slowly throughout the night from a plethora of sources. Gurgles in one's throat from malnourishment reflux, drippings from irritated nostrils repelling all senses invading its canals, foul sweat oozing from every conceivable millimeter of a contorted homo sapien in repose. The womb itself mirrors the instability of its invader as its porous fissures weep tears of humidity.

Throughout the night various multi-pedal creatures of indeterminate lineage can be felt harvesting upon the carcass with varying degrees of intensity. Upon detection, it attempts to thwart their appetite with a flick here, a fist there - only to detect the reverberation of their many feet scurrying away to regroup and reattack, while it grows increasingly unawares as night bans entry to its consciousness. A welcome deflection from a world of incessant cacophony above, below and within.

No matter the setting of one's nocturnal repose – it is by and large the great equalizer. The weight of night gracefully settles upon humanity's collective scale, resetting the imbalances of any day for all. A singular flatline quieting the conscious and subconscious of every breathing being, until morning's revival. Can one discern upon looking into another's eyes upon waking whether or not they have traveled to other worlds through the course of the night? A fatigue born of bliss or of trepidation conceived in ever present anxieties?

Daylight pricks the womb, expelling its contents clumsily into a new day. Eyes rubbed, conscious restored, it puts one foot ahead of another in an unintentional direction. The digital neon clock continues to tick away - like a bomb whose fuse length is known only to the universe glaring downwards from above with merciless indifference.

Batalla by Rene Ujlenhoet

The one great continuity of my life, aside from the frame in which I am compelled to reside within from first gasp to last, is the sound of Church bells. They broadcasted to the village that my father had at last, after several arduous trials and tribulations, managed to snare a heart who henceforth would be known by no other name than his. Soon thereafter, their union produced one of several replicas of their combined physical attributes – diced, tossed and lovingly stirred for nine months in evolution's cauldron - before being served up for scrutiny to a gaggle of gossips at my Christening. Another successful procreation, jubilantly heralded for all to bask in its predicted future glory. I wonder how many today recall where they were on that auspicious day aside from those whose duty it is to remember such milestones?

As time wore on the bells seemed to ring less often and with ever diminishing luster. After all, many abandoned the village for the wiles of city life - while others headed the calls for war. Still, childhood memories of births, weddings, funerals, holidays and routine Sunday calls to prayer resonated in the heart's memories of one and all no matter how far and wide we were scattered about the earth.

I was one of those who wandered through many a land as the calls to war came one after another in a seemingly endless torrent of commands from hilltop palaces above to poor villages below. One campaign led to another and another, taking young men like me further and further from the peals of our homes - their melodies ringing softly in tandem with the peaks and troughs of our every breath during sleepless nights on foreign soils awaiting bloody dawns. The memories accompanying the ringing in our hearts were largely a typical mixture of sweet and somber associations born of our individual pasts nested in our collective humanity. Nevertheless, despite shared familiarities upon the paths whereby we converged here, we never spoke of our pasts. Each of us knew that the next ringing of bells back home may very well be in recognition of our own departures from this world. It was an ever-present possibility best left locked away from the prying eyes and finely tuned ears of contemplation - lest ones blindness in war were suddenly to be lifted. Seeing the enemy as a reflection rather than as an inversion would likely loosen one's grip upon one's sword leading to an earlier than necessary departure.

Laying awake, staring at the stars, bells ringing in my ears, I began to contemplate whether or not the resonance of bells is be indistinguishable to most. Whether marking a happy occasion or sad, a typical Sunday mass or the funeral of a loved one – I can attest to the indisputable fact that bell tones are as alike as snowflakes. For me, it's not so much a matter of what course the audible stream takes as it enters the ear canal, it's how its essence transforms the soul which makes each clang an unequivocally individual experience - often incapable of accurate description by even the bearer of the soul in whose lodgings it has reverberated.

For example, one witnessing a tear from a distance can never fully appreciate the taste of salt upon the lips of the bereaved, the tightening in their chest from choking on despair, as eyelids refuse entry to the reality of void requesting permission to land upon their conscious. The heavy drone from bells above resounding to the bearer below will forever resound as an echo dipping into a bottomless well dredged by unfathomable grief. A hollow tone continuously playing on loop in one's subconscious – occasionally surfacing to the conscious in a quest for expulsion from memory altogether by means of becoming snagged by a fishhook cast by time into oblivion.

In contrast, on the opposing shore of life's waterways lie harmonious bells heralding inexplicable happiness. The bride who sees herself reflected in her husband's eyes – a luminous, impenetrable circle embracing her likeness woven of his eternal devotion to her and her alone. His dumbstruck silence at the beauty who chose him and him alone - when she could have had her pick amongst millions deemed worthier in the eyes of well-meaning meddlers.

The husband receiving his newly soaked progeny in his arms as a beam of Heaven's light gently strokes its tiny head in consolation for all the commotion. The parents, relieved to herald a continuation of their line. When the final bell strikes for them, it will signify a snipped branch, not a felled tree.

Retiring to drafty tents, we restlessly seek solace on damp ground. All are asleep, yet keenly awake at the snap of every twig, the whisper of every wind. I close a curtain on the present by nestling in the past, focusing keenly on the bells that have rung for my family and I through good times and bad. Each ring a reminder of presence in an otherwise forgetful, anonymous world. Between battles one spends an inordinate amount of time sitting around campfires waiting for time to pass until the next ordered slaughter. Many back home think these are times full of drinking and reminiscing about families and lovers among other various frivolities. After a day's battle, it's silence that reigns, with only the crackling fire striking up monotonous chatter. What's past is past, no one seeks to relive the snatching of souls out from under life that has rained misery upon yet another blood-soaked day. Apathy is the key to keeping madness at bay.

As I look about, I wonder if others too hear bells in their slumber to quiet the storms surging in their conscious. Do they hear bells of weddings – their own and of kin? Or bells of order – marking the end of another successfully completed week as they renew their life pass for yet another? Some appear content, while others discomforted. Perhaps by memories of a loss from which they fled, only to find one can never outrun one's shadow.

And what of those whose morning will be cut short? In villages to be raided, the very same bells from which we have sprung will ring out in terror of what is to come. Throughout the siege their collective clamor will muffle wave after wave of imploring vocalizations:

Erupting cries springing from wells of heroism hoping to erase fate's ink before it dries and rewrite their course;

Mothers on their knees pleading for mercy - attempting to light a match before our shuttered eyes to dispel the darkness within us;

The wailing of bereavement slowly encroaching upon an otherwise sunny afternoon, wrapping all in its wake in a cloak of weighty chains from which few will ever find respite.

After our passing, those few who remain will solemnly strike bells one at a time, intermittently, for the ascension of those whose voices have been exiled towards lands – fathomable, but uncharted. A toxic brew of bells, shock and grief fermenting in one's conscious distorts otherwise familiar sounds into alien projections that seize the heart one stabbing beat at a time while blinding one's vision – both inner and outer – with a thick torrent of grief that, for most, will eventually evaporate into pure, distilled hate.

They will never know a moment's peace as memory and pain take turns pounding away at their very souls – re-opening every wound, no matter how small, every day for as long as they can recall those who occupied the now empty chairs at their tables. The swirling cacophony engulfing their conscious and subconscious lives back and forth and simultaneously like a seesaw of saws will cease only when a final, singular bell is rung external to their inner world, signaling that their mortal life has itself expired.

As they journey into the hereafter, clamor is pounded into submission by the coalesced forces of all things divine. What was once a parasitic ringing buzzing about their souls is expelled as they enter the outer cosmos. Having fallen at their feet in defeat, all mortal torments morph into a silken pathway in penance for all they unleashed below.

Finding peace at last, the soul is repaired, polished, and kissed anew. After a well-earned respite it will be re-purposed to make the return trip home, accompanied by new and joyous bells greeting its arrival -as the final bell tolls for me.

Panayiotis Kokoras – Cycling

The vast blue cauldron whose breadth and depth stretched beyond what any mortal eye could see - opened its mouth to receive a treat. Angels and sprites flowing and flitting to and fro playfully chasing insomniac stars refusing to be put to bed, as day's rays pulled the curtains back when dawn began knocking. One by one they tugged at, tackled, tickled and tossed the giggling sparks into the cool blue broth. Tomorrow was to be no ordinary day. Winter was checking in, due to stay for several months - as wished for by eager little boys and girls, bored with belly flop slides through sticky fall foliage.

A grand procession was planned. Select stars shedding their luminous coats, revealing lacey underclothes – no two alike – plainly visible to all who care to notice. In their millions they will somersault from the giant cauldron onto all below in a shower smudging out even the slightest sliver of sky.

A cascade of joy – flakes playfully jostling to catch the swiftest currents as others admire their twirls and swirls from above and alongside. Others snuggling together for the downward slide, anxious about where they'll land below.

Some land atop one another in a giant heap. Others land soundly, only to be tossed aloft again by an unforeseen gust. A precious few never land at all as they melt upon impact when snatched by the tongues of cheeky children having fun.

The subtle, constant chatter of ice tossing and turning brings nostalgia to the old, wonderment to the young and hope to many more. After all, when gathered on mass, snowflakes have the uncanny ability to hush the noisiest of cities, and blanket the dirtiest of environments with a white sheet of erasure - in their heaped unity, gently hinting at the possibility of writing a new and better chapter.

"К" for Bass Flute and Violin by Anna Pospelova

Swipe left, swipe left, swipe left. Carpel tunnel is setting
in. I mean seriously, the app says a ton of potentials are
swimming right here in this watering hole just waiting for
my lure!   A third are men and it estimates approximately
20% of them are single. What about the other 80%? I'll
bet they have a ring jingling in their back pocket -
hopefully a homing beacon for a lighting strike looking for
a conduit as they walk to their car without me.
Swipe left, swipe left…maybe…maybe….ah no, the pic is
fake - no one can be that flawless without photoshop. No,
no, in your dreams, oh please…only a mother could love,
too fat, too thin, too bald, too hairy, bad teeth, pop eyes,
buzzard nose, dumbo ears.

He sees the fawn amidst the hops. His sight closes in on
none but her as slowly, slowly his heart unlocks the door
and, with enormous trepidation, peeks. His heart bursts
forth at warp speed gallop. Having reached her heart, it
knocks persistently hoping for entry.

Startled from her monotony by a fateful tickle in her chest,
at last she glances upward and is immediately entranced.
Arrows are launched, received and relaunched in kind by
rollicking Cupids in their respective pupil's deep trenches.

Summoning up courage from wells as yet untapped, he
parts the sea before him to slowly make his way over to
her – nary a coherent thought brewing in his head for his
tongue to offer upon arrival. He gently snapped the ice
with a succession of light questions – name, job and the
ever so reliable weather volley when silence threatens

defeat. With gushing enthusiasm she returned his serve in rhythmic fashion chiming in with cheerful retorts, witty repartees and the occasional genteel giggle – to which he responded in kind with nods, smiles and just a word or two so as not to hog the covers as they say.

Awkward first steps aside, they soon find their stride. Conversation flows as smoothly as a swan gently gliding round and round a pond stuffed with billowy sky cotton. Two become one as their hearts exchange secret codes, unlocking all within. His hand in hers and hers in his, they enter each others eyes for a look around - making space in their cognitive armoires for the other's thoughts, casting aside ones of themselves. At the very last, they sync their internal clocks – those vital mechanisms which intuitively ring so as one is never late to fulfill any needs of the other whether great or small. At the end of the meeting, they open the door and step into destiny, leaving but one set of footprints in their wake.

Circular Bowing Study by Angharad Davies

Every day begins and ends with erasure. Upon waking I
rub my face over and over again with water to erase
sleep's debris. In the kitchen I collect the remnants of
slaughtered plants and animals – sausage, eggs and orange
juice in order to replenish my interior space, which has
already expelled what came before it. As soon as it
appears before me, I erase the plate one element at a
time.
Once again in the bathroom, I go over and over my teeth
with a fine-toothed comb to expel all evidence of what I've
just done in the kitchen. Water is probably one of the
most commonly used elements in our daily lives for
expunging impurities. Ironic that a principal agent of
erasure also makes up sixty percent of our body mass, and
yet our conscience is never completely spotless no matter
how ruthlessly we scrub it – just ask Lady Macbeth.

After a shower, I rub the condensation from the mirror
over and over again hoping my age spots surrender or at
least retreat. Weary of battle, it is I who retreats from the
wall of reflection which steadfastly refuses to appease my
entreaties with a simple white lie – you are still the fairest
of them all. An innocuous trifle of a crumb for which
practically everyone would be willing to sacrifice their soul.

The well-trodden path to work – so predictable one could
do it blindfolded. What is red is reversed to green and vice
versa in a steady hum that is the pulse of conventional life.
During the course of the morning energy is expelled in a
litany of e-mails, reports and voice mails. All erased in the

course of an afternoon as e-mails are trashed, voice mails deleted and old reports shredded. Over the course of years and years of work in a multitude of environments, one is never remembered. All your output has been recycled or discarded bit by bit until you yourself are no longer present either, save for a vague memory or two from those who bothered to notice you.

As age starts beating you in the race for mortality, your consciousness of purpose begins eroding even before you initiate the most mundane of tasks. The rear-view mirror of life becomes increasingly obscured by time as memories dissipate at an ever-increasing rate, despite your fervent attempts to restore its clarity by rubbing it with your frail fingers. Even the road ahead is little more than a hazy present in which more and more sounds, colors and bustling of life around you become fainter as a transparent shroud slowly makes its way over your being until your life is erased in its entirety.

Ring by Aisha Orbazayeva

Swaddled snuggly in a basket to the side, a babe watches in awe as a bulging sack of rumpled cloth topped with a silvery pelt cozily settles into a familiar heap of readiness alongside. An alter stands before her anchored by earth and sky - the rays within beckoning for colors only she can conjure.

Deftly manipulating both warp and batten like any experienced conductor, she guides ancestral colors along traditional pathways - in and out, over and under. At the end of the road, she tucks them in with the gentleness of a new mother, securing their place before extending an open palm to those waiting to traverse.

A hush envelops the room as heart to heart, babe to elder - an unbreakable bond as delicate as a spider's web spun from love unfolds. With each passing row, colors familiar to the hearts of experienced creators once again take stage in the present, proceeding through their guiding hands in becoming a foundation upon which future generations, both those in process of maturation and those as yet unarrived, can marvel.

Once completed, the elder smiles with satisfaction, winking at the babe who in turn immediately spots the opening left behind. A light-colored patch amidst the sea of dark. As the Spider Woman legend demands of all her progeny – an opening is always left to allow the energy of the work to escape the confines of the rug. A portal through which love and respect can be both given and received.

Piolin by José Julio Díaz Infante

Glacial shifts begin imperceptibly. Temperatures rise a few degrees. Internal constrictions ease just enough to precipitate a drip. An amalgam ensues of thoughtful and thoughtless words casually tossed back and forth across a topic. As temperatures continue to rise, drips converge into trickles. Non-participants in the original match begin to observe and keep score. As with all experiences governed by the fickleness of variability, one side quickly outpaces the other.

Rising temperatures increase more rapidly. What was once a trickle is now an audible torment branching out indiscriminately creating fractures through friction, rendering solidarity a myth shrugged off by most. Only a few recognize the signs and sounds of division. Even fewer muster the courage to call for hostilities to halt - armed with nothing more than reasoning, futilely blasting point after point into dense, vapid air as others cower in silent resignation. If only the mute could speak to the blind. The pregnant pause has not borne fruit, fracturing resumes as all resistance fades.

A few quietly slide down crevasses, disconnecting themselves entirely from the situation at hand – never to be seen, heard from or thought of again – as if their lives were never lived beyond their initial introduction. Others leap from the scene with dramatic flair, crashing into the wilds below, igniting wave upon wave forewarning of days of discontent likely to spread to even the furthest shores.

With all resistance constrained or evaporated, the fissures coalesce into common purpose as they render their own home of thousands of years asunder until there remains nothing more than a single droplet in a sea of regret.

Inwendig losgelöst By Wolfgang Mitterer

Whitling away the hours of any day, a pedantic collector strolled murky shores in search of hidden treasure. Neither gold nor gems, that could have belonged to anyone living beyond their means, were to his liking. It was remnants of personal intention he craved. Those items which extended one beyond one's mortality, or simply marked a singular experience whose worthiness is enshrined in some way to satiate their need to stake claim to relevance in a crowded field of life – either for future personal reflection and commemoration, or for public benefit and admiration.

Unlike other scavengers, he detested metal detectors. There was personal satisfaction in retrieving life from the mud with one's bare hands. He likened it to birth, except in this case it was re-birth of sentiments once lived – how impersonal if one were to exhume them with tools!

Down sank his nimble fingers into the enveloping sands of time, extending an offering of daylight to elements having for so long slumbered in darkness. A pebble here, algae there, until at last something crafted by man takes the bait, rising to the occasion at hand.

From a handful of sludge emerges a timeless silver coated oyster. After a quick dip in the traffic of salty water hurling by his feet, he uses his longest fingernail to pry open its tiny mouth. Behold! His first glimpse into the past is a reflection of the present as he sees nothing other than his own peering pupil. If only he could turn the tiny tarnished mirror backwards to reflect its past possessor, what delight would be had! One could easily imagine a rosy cheeked maiden pinching, propping and perspiring while prepping for her very first ball.

Did the mirror hold the gaze of a singular admirer, upon whose demise it was banished to the rubbish heaps of antiquity? Perhaps it was a constant companion of the maiden throughout her life? In subsequent years this selfsame mirror would have kept those very same eyes company - albeit tucked into the creases of a very different face. One stretched by time, weathered by disappointments, whose eyes nonetheless glow with memories of better days gone by.

When does one discard so precious an object? Something so intimate that it alone knows every secret of the soul peering at it - yet steadfastly reveals nothing to anyone outside its beholder. Such loyalty is unheard of amongst the animate. Perhaps upon dissolution of its owner, the mirror itself fogs, cracks and distorts out of fidelity to its beloved. It can bear to reflect none other.

A treasure to be treasured to the discoverer to be sure. The search begins anew. Sloshing and swishing through smelly mud, one often surfaces little more than sludge. Weeks if not months can pass before you find something of interest at last, but well worth the wait. Just have a look at this old pipe about which a shoal of tiny fish were circling round and round as if emanating from its core as smoke once did. One wonders at what point in time man conjured such a contraption to capture and regulate the flow of willfully inhaled carcinogens?

Whose hands picked the calabash gourd from which it was fashioned? Whose lips were on the receiving end of its birth? Was it a young man gasping on his first gulp of manhood, or perhaps even a woman sneaking a forbidden whiff? More than likely given its pedigree, it would have belonged to a man with many years under his belt and an overflowing wallet in his pocket.

He probably puffed away on it in a gentlemen's club of some sort in full view of as many patrons as possible who could admire the expense of the object in hand and assume said wealth traversed through to the personage upon whose lips it perched. What irony it would be if it were all a ruse! That the pipe in hand were in reality a relic from the family war chest – pilfered in times of financial tailspin in hopes of hanging on to the last thread of propriety tethering them to the milieu to which they had grown so accustomed and attached.

If only one could resurrect the past by placing one's lips upon the present and with a gentle inhalation expel the genie from the calabash shell, demanding it spill its lore. What tales it could tell of heated whispers and outright brawls crackling beneath its lethargic, ethereal strolls towards the low ceilings of musty, mahogany dens bursting at the seams with privileged iniquity. Pathetic panderers groveling for patronage, pernicious politicians dolling out pettiness to any bored enough to listen and of course outright scandals of the upper crust sneakily rummaging about for crumbs under the table! Alas, if only smoke could talk, what tales could be told!

Speaking of tales, one is reminded of the ladies fan steadfastly closed to prying eyes. Once rinsed of time and massaged with cleansing agents did it begin to telegraph tales of long ago.

Probably dating from Victorian times one could imagine a whole gaggle of giggling girls fishing at a ball. Some well and truly innocent, others so beyond the pale that mere mention of their name alone would elicit a gasp. They were the most fascinating to observe – true masters of their craft.

Like unsheathing a sword they would wield their fan with frightening dexterity. Scanning the room, identifying prey – as soon as it returned her stare, the trap was laid. She'd place a closed fan such as this right next to her heart and with a sly smile let him know he was the chosen one. What man can resist such a message as that? Touching a slat such as this very first one, she'd convey the message that he and he alone could compel her to reveal all. Slat by slat, lace unfurling as seductively as ripples in a moonlit pond – the anticipation must have been tremendous. Slowly, slowly slat by slat – how he must have trembled wondering how many there were to go. The heat so intense, his collar all but soaked, would all be unfurled or would she be a tease and fold all back to the beginning when they had only reached halfway? Slat by slat, hope by hope, two merging into one as the sun submitted to the darkness coaxing it from below. For the occasional victors, all slats would be laid bare as she retired into the cold air of evening, lying in wait for him to come nearer.

If one were to consider the opposite end of that spectrum, one might contemplate the pilgrim's medallion that disembarked with the tide on a cold winter's day just as the sun arose. Although well worn by penitent hands rubbing it for luck long before the sands of time took their toll, it appears to be Thomas Beckett top his horse, gallantly trotting through merry England well before his grisly murder. Pilgrims to Canterbury sought these tokens as amulets of hope in times of despair, illness or more than likely in the hopes that flashing such bling would be your ticket to esteem amongst your peers - despite the fact it would fall well short of what you'd have to pony up for a ticket to heaven given your less than pious past. The intrigue lies in guessing of which ilk our penitent parishioner fell into.

Speaking of humanity's incessant prostrations towards a self-created invisibly manifested divinity, feast your eyes upon this miniature equine. Crudely made of clay, one cannot help but pantomime a mighty gallop when straddling it in one's palm, no matter one's age. The sensation of a hoof immediately brings to mind thundering clumps of earth being wildly tossed into the air, leaving a distinct trail in its wake. Even when in miniature, the images conjured upon perusal of its form immediately bring to mind grandeur and daring well in excess of its tiny frame.

Yes, it is probably something as simple as a child's toy. However, it isn't an impossibility to embrace the possibility of it being an offering to an ancient polytheistic god – perhaps even a replica of the god itself. Whether a manifestation of divinity or a past time of youth, it is beyond doubt that it possessed intangible value – the most priceless commodity of all.

From effigy to entrapment, let us consider an insect trapped in an amber amulet. A mumification of torment worn as jewelry. One can but imagine the insect's sense of doom upon realization of its delicate legs being mired in the viscous, golden goo. How it must have struggled in those final moments to free itself. Although animals don't possess the ability to reflect – at least not in the way to which we are accustomed – it most certainly preferred life over death, as all animals do.

How the owner of the amulet must have admired the amber hue and probably marveled at the intactness of its hostage. She couldn't begin to fathom what the world was like back in the era in to which this tiny insect was witness, so very long ago. Now, all that remains of a first-hand account of times long past, is the agony of its last breath, petrified for the present. An agonizing reminder that what truly binds all creatures great and small, no matter their time or place, is an innate desire to persist to the last drop of our strength.

In his last will and testament, our intrepid collector has dutifully noted that all of his treasures be bequeathed back into the embrace of the river from which they were reborn, so future generations strolling along these gentle shores may be drawn into their depths to seek its stories yet again. The stories of imagined people from long past places whose sole connection to us lay in a shared species designation and the capacity to connect through the ages with one another by way of what we are not – inanimate things.

Alveoles for String Quartet by Santa Ratniece

Sirens slithering amongst opaque, coal infused shallows beckon the brightest of all stars to its embrace in the guise of twilight. Smooth, silky voices so minutely perceptible that one strains to hear their refrains - as if hunting for a spider's web in a snow drenched field beneath blinding midday rays.

Shall we avert our eyes from the struggle of a giant against an undefeatable, invisible enemy? After all, we too are up against an invincible foe – time. It's simply that the trajectory of our struggle is more drawn out. Therefore, while we pity the giant's demise, there is a bit of jealousy in knowing, unlike us, it will arise unscathed to breathe again in the same form to which it has become accustomed.

All hear the call of sirens at some point in their lives. Consider the starving man deliriously wandering lost in the undulating coils of a desert under perpetual siege by that selfsame unforgiving, fire-breathing star. He may very well at times welcome its reckoning - hoping in vain for its rebirth to be aborted. Nevertheless, as it rises again, he does not emulate its brief capitulation to the siren's call for submission, but rather takes from its resurrection hope that everyone possesses the possibility of rebirth from constriction.

Transformation abounds in sync with siren melodies. Just as oceans swell and wane, so life undulates between variable extremes each and every day.

Workers return to familial wombs, lovers into the arms of loved ones, roosters to roosts. Herbs harvested and livestock sacrificed make their way into pots and pans to be rendered into fuel for those in their wake who, despite their ensuing absence, will surge forward to grasp another day.

Sirens continue to beckon even amongst the folds of blinding night in the dreams of young and old, friend and foe, animals and sprites. All descend to lands frightful or fantastic, only to emerge alongside our one flaming star as morning tears curtains asunder, as we anticipate unchartered journeys to come. All until our very last moment, when hailed by those selfsame sirens we realize our life is well and truly done.

Guro Moe – Short Piece for Octobass

As Apollo's jaws began to loosen, man reflected more poignantly than ever before on his timeline. Having not so long ago originated as little more than a hairless ape who could barely stand upright, let alone communicate to this – one step away from frolicking in the dust of a sphere hundreds of thousands of miles above his own.

For those gawking below to those waiting to exit – anticipation and trepidation sloshed about as inversely proportionate waves engulfing all from head to toe. Through the ever-widening crack in Apollo's side - silence reigned. A silence so thick as to deafen all senses into a hypnotic emptiness - melting all thoughts and emotions into a singular, wordless stare.

A giant step would soon be taken – the first of its kind in all of history. And yet, as the window to the future widens further and further so as to enable such a step to emerge through its void and make its mark upon the new world laying patiently in its path - the astronaut within is held breathless more by what lay in his wake. For just before landing, he had peered out this very same window and looked back towards the planet from which he came. A mass of lapis swirled through clouds. Never had it seemed so perfect until it lay in the past. The lifeless, grey dust awaiting him seemed a step behind rather than forwards.

Perhaps the real message for the betterment of mankind lay in reflection, rather than projection of what is possible in a borderless land.

Alfred Schnittke Concerto Grosso No.1 for 2 Violins Rondo

Scheherazade tossed and turned upon waves of satin. Anxiously wandering through a thicket of thorns, her gaze is suddenly snared by a gazelle. Its coal black eyes constantly capturing any beauty beheld in its world and reflecting it in turn – thereby igniting any soul fortunate enough to have stumbled into the chance of attracting its fleeting glance.

Mesmerized by her encounter, she is startled by its sudden flight. Intrinsic to humanity is its thirst to possess. Once intoxicated by an encounter, they'll stop at nothing to prolong the moment as long as possible - thereby denying it to all others.

As it fled from her path, she initiated a pursuit. Their slender limbs twisted and turned amongst the trees with the fluidity of rivulets braiding one another's strands on a warm summer's eve. With flawless grace, the gazelle pranced up slopes - not unlike Pegasus parting a path through buxom clouds with its mighty wings.

Scheherazade's energy was waning as she struggled to keep pace. However, there was no question of quitting, for this was the ultimate race.

How many have pursued the greatest of muses in the deepest thickets of imagination, only to see a lifetime expire without so much as a glance?

Thrice did the Gazelle pause for a quick breath and scan of what lay before, beyond and behind. Thriving on the thrill of being pursued, it wanted to prolong the adventure for as long as possible - never did it pursue smothering its own tracks.

As seconds turned minutes into hours Scheherazade's pace slowed under the harnesses of Ra's rays. A mossy knoll cradled by shade bid her lay down for a brief repose. And there she lay, nestled in its moist embrace - all the while gazing at upwards towards the torrent of light spilling from heaven's lamp. What a wonder to behold! Such magic unveiled by the universe's sole instrument of illumination.

How lovely would it be to rub its golden belly on a whim and be granted all in this world and beyond that one could imagine? For certain she wasn't the first to ponder the possibility - many a child and autocrat must have mulled it before her. After all, is there anyone immune from the tug-o-war between admiration and envy when contemplating that ever-present, untouchable golden star whose fire can never be harnessed or extinguished?

The gazelle sheepishly tip-toed nearer its pursuer out of curiosity. Scheherazade, still intoxicated by the radiant golden rapture, failed to notice until an apple dislodged from above thumped her on the head with a Newtonian thump. Cured of any delirium, she spotted the gazelle close by and suddenly hungered yet again to reignite the chase.

Light as a dandelion bouncing upon a breeze, the gazelle skipped from rock to rock through the middle of a creek with the greatest of ease. Scheherazade, determined to keep pace leapt into the water with far less grace. The mounds of cloth swaddling her tiny frame rapidly gained weight as they greedily gulped all engulfing it. Frantically she tried to grab onto a rock, but was pushed away. The current and gravity fought like jealous lovers to embrace her alone. Both pulling her downstream and downwards. She swirled and swirled, twirling as if in a waltz whose grip wouldn't loosen until her very breath ran out.

At last tossed upon the bank, as all were exhausted from tussling, she awoke later on like a lump of mud upon the shore - face to face yet again with the Gazelle.

When assured all was well, up the hill it sprang. Scheherazade watched it ascend to what appeared to be a golden den.

If ever there were a thief's paradise upon the earth, this was it. It took no more than a single spider's thread-worth of sunlight to illuminate the fire within. A golden womb carved out of a mountain's belly, snuggling all seeking sheltering within from the rapids of life outside of it.

Although she was curious to enter, there was also something foreboding about a concealed maze for which one had no map – no matter how enticing it seemed. What for one may be an adventure, for another could mean disaster when exploring all that lies within. After all - the deeper you go, the dimmer the light. When practically all external sensory processing is abated, one's only remaining companions are wit and hope.

Scheherazade suddenly awoke to a new day and destiny. Her journey through the forests of her own imagination with the Gazelle as her guiding muse had given her the key to bring the Sultan to his knees. Summoning her father, she confidently declared, "I will be his last and outlasting bride."

Iannis Xenakis – Mikka

It hovered just beyond his reach, not unlike his mother-in-laws ceaseless demands - and was equally as pointless. Its entire mass expanding well under an inch and weighing no more than a few milligrams. Usually you don't even notice it, but when you do, you're possessed with a passion to pursue - unrivaled by even a goddess on a visitor's visa from heaven.

There is an old proverb, "a single person in a field doesn't make a warrior", which of course Western civilization sexualized (as it does practically everything) into "it takes two to tango" – robbing it of any chivalric notion whatsoever. Whether it is one person or thousands congregated in a space, this tiny insect can enrage all within its sights by simply reminding them it shares their space.

I firmly believe it does a fly by within earshot as the first tease. It probably picked up on the technique from watching men whisper sweet nothings into women's ears and decided to be just as bold. Then, like an anxious lover, it hovers in front of you waiting for a reaction. Except, what it wants is from you is to strike out at it - just as David egged on Goliath.

From the beginning of time until its inevitable end, can there be a greater irony aside from the fact that the greater the breadth of inverse proportionality between two breathing beings – in terms of space consumed and courage stored - the greater the need for the dominate space consumer to destroy the latter, no matter the cost in dignity.

Nina Shekar – Hush

Rain drops parting cumulus clouds, gently poking holes in Heaven's vault to make way for the coming of Luna's celestial illumination. Peeking between autumn's deciduous fingers, it bathes a glistening egg in brightness, as a chick will soon begin its ascent onto the stage of life.

Moist from a mother's underbelly, its pristine surface extols to any bearing witness the irrefutability of its utter perfection in both texture and shape. A marvel of creation bearing no signature.

Despite the warmth in its calcium cradle, the chick cannot help but be tempted to source the glow bathing its inner darkness in light. Soon it will be time to burst through the womb, making its way towards an unknowable destiny - aside from a certainty of unconditional maternal love. Guaranteed despite its origins from a cuckoo skulking away betwixt the full moon's rays.

"K" for Bass Flute and Violin by Anna Pospelova (Revisited)

Odorous expulsions from above and below, punctuated by intermittent wails of discontent, discomfort, distraction or delight in varying degrees of pitch and length – the sole commonality of which lays in the fact that the motivation behind each vocalization is unintelligible to all but the owner of the larynx from which they are launched.

Its sense of directionality seems akin to that of a vacuum ingesting all its path while making sense of none of it – diamond earrings and a dropped paper clip being deemed of equal value.

Such an enormous distance its tiny eyes must travel from the floor all the way up my height of over six foot. One would think that would inspire a sense of awe, especially when I am issuing reprimands over its latest misadventure. Instead, when our eyes finally meet, my exasperation is met with a bundle of giggles let loose by flaying hands tugging at my hem in a plea to play. Despite no acquiescence play is at hand as it slides across the carpet hanging onto my drool-soaked ankle as in vain I attempt to extricate myself from the result of my surrender to passion.

Soon bored with the ride, it lets go only to snort, sniffle, gurgle and gulp yet again. It spots a plush toy and is at last engaged. Pulling its ears, poking its belly, chewing on its nose, rolling on top of it, throwing it against a wall then starting all over again.

Only when I lay it in an open cage do both of us score a reprieve. As I watch it peacefully slide into its imagination, I marvel at how something so petite can have such boundless energy when awake. Now and then, it runs its hands subconsciously along the rails, sensing the openings here and there. I'm sure come morning it will consider the possibility of escape an irresistible dare.

I suppose one must conclude – despite all the chaos – that given a few decades all will pay off. Like any artist who has splattered paints or tapped pens for hours on end on blank pages, one must take into account that despite that one in a million chance of creating a masterpiece, if you manage to pull it off, that one night of passion and subsequent decades of toil will have been rewarded in kind by your immortalization in the annuals of time by those who will be grateful you consented.

I am Not a Clockmaker Either by Ann Cleare

The wooden planks slapped the gentle river at an ever-
quickening pace. Churning the world below into a tornadic
chaos of unnatural bubbling, swells and blindsiding
currents – fish either scattered in its wake or watched
from afar in bewildered curiosity.

The cacophony was mirrored above:
      kitchen doors slamming open and shut,
          mops swishing back and forth along decks
             drenched in river sweat,
      silverware plunked down on the finest linen,
windows vigorously scrubbed to squeak when noses
pressed
         against them,
     maids whimsically swiping ivory keyboards from end
to end each time they pass by,
         chefs busily lacerating the finest meats and
            hardiest vegetables while swishing
   dazzling whirlpools of blood red sauces in boiling hot
pans.
      The domino-scurry of rambunctious children's feet
         winding their way around the boat's waist.

As they were squeezed into narrowing waters, crowds
gathered along the shore. Faces popping like popcorn
between shoulders and legs with a few wayward hands
eliciting an occasional gasp or laugh depending upon the
recipient.

Time presses on despite a constant winding of clocks on board. Upon morning they were set back to make all think they were ahead of schedule, and upon evening set forward to give the servants a respite from passenger demands after an excruciating day.

Pushing against contrary currents, the boat continued to rip through the heart of the country, leaving a divided spectatorship to eye one another across an ever-widening moat. 1918 was but five years away.

Keep Digging the Hare Hole by Sofia Avramidou

Nudging the glass between my lips, allowing the water therein to trickle into the abyss - I imagine my consciousness hitching a ride in the folds of its current, setting off to explore the unfamiliar laying within my very familiar frame.

I expected an almost immediate plunge from head to toe rather than the slow, undulating meanderings through warrens of pipes, thick and thin, crisscrossing like cabs taking drunken passengers on overly extended routes home in hopes of rendering them penniless come morning when they awaken delirious on their doorsteps.

Unlike all the films you watched in school as a child, there is no sensation of bold reds and snuggly pinks. All is darkness protectively ensconced in skin. Despite the absence of conventional light – the exposure of all that makes you…you, lay within every millimeter over which you are passing.

Memories of all that has transpired since your inception are not archived as they are on the outside by purely visual encapsulations in stills and films. Like rings in a tree, they are physically sensed as you sense indentations wrought by circumstances both physical and emotional.

Hairline interruptions in otherwise smooth bones from where they were once cracked,

A rise in the sea level of acids when attacked by nerves or gluttony,

Hair follicles rotting at their roots from age or sudden stress,

Enlarged hearts from loving too much,
        shrunken ones from loving too little.

One continues to traverse at dizzying speeds down slick luge tracks, gaining G force as the emotional soundtrack of the life you've lived thus far re-exerts itself into your current conscious. One is exploding with exhilaration over all triumphs great and small and constricting all senses in avoidance of the directly proportional desire to cross into death to relieve the regret of all that might have been, but will never be. Only a few will manage to turn their backs to Styx's sirens beckoning and rise like phoenixes to meet the challenge of another day.

Manufactured by Amazon.ca
Acheson, AB

11928861R00057